Sandy Goes to the Vet

Story by Dawn McMillan

Illustrations by Liz Alger

Rigby

A Harcourt Achieve Imprint

www.Rigby.com

1-800-531-5015

Harry went to see his pet rabbit.

"Here are some carrots for you,
Sandy," he said.
"You like carrots!"

Sandy did not eat the carrots.

He hopped slowly
over to his little house
and went inside.

Harry ran to get Dad.

"Sandy is not eating his carrots!"
he said. "Is he sick?"

"I will come and take a look
at him," said Dad.

Dad went with Harry
to see Sandy.

"Look!" said Harry.
"Sandy's ears are way down!"

"His nose is hot and dry, too,"
said Dad. "He **is** sick."

"Let's take him to the vet,"
said Harry.
"I will get a box from the shed."

Dad opened the car door.

Harry said,
"We are going to the vet, Sandy."

The vet took Sandy out of the box.

"Come on, little rabbit," she said.

"Sit up here, on the table."

The vet looked at Sandy.

"Oh dear!" she said.

"You **are** sick!"

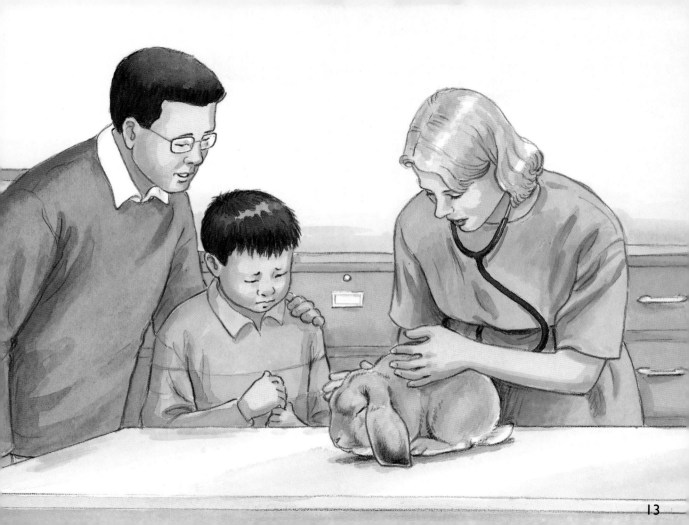

"This will make Sandy better,"
said the vet.
"In a day or two,
  he will be eating his carrots
and hopping in the garden!"

"That's good!" said Harry.

"Then I can play with him again."